W9-CKH-979

Walt Disney's
Winnie the Pooh
AND
THE LITTLE LOST BIRD

By BETTY BIRNEY
Illustrated by RUSSELL HICKS

A GOLDEN BOOK • NEW YORK
Western Publishing Company, Inc., Racine, Wisconsin 53404

It was a beautiful spring day, the kind of day that made Winnie the Pooh want to skip and sing.

But as he skipped through the Hundred-Acre Wood, his song was interrupted by a loud sound:

"Cheep! Cheep! CHEEP!"

Pooh followed the sound and found a nest. Inside the nest was a very tiny, very loud, blue baby bird.

"*Cheep!*" said the bird.

"*Cheep* to you, too. My name is Pooh," said Pooh. Then he laughed. "Oh, I made a poem."

Pooh took another look at the bird. "You're too little to fly, aren't you?" said Pooh. "And you can't stay here all alone on the ground. You need food and a home. I'll take you home with me."

When they got home, Pooh told his new friend, "I'll call you Baby Blue, because Blue rhymes with Pooh!"

Pooh thought Baby Blue looked hungry, so he offered her some honey. But Baby Blue didn't seem to like it nearly as much as Pooh did.

Later that day Piglet brought over a whole basket of haycorns for Baby Blue. But she didn't seem to like haycorns nearly as much as Piglet did.

Rabbit brought Baby Blue his biggest, juiciest carrot. But Baby Blue didn't like the carrot at all.

Finally they found some birdseed, and Baby Blue gobbled it up.

In a corner of Pooh's house, Eeyore helped Pooh make a soft bed and a tiny chair for Baby Blue. They even hung a little picture of Baby Blue's new friends.

"You'll be safe living here, Baby Blue," Pooh said. "Much safer than in a nest."

Baby Blue sat in her own special corner, but she didn't look happy.

Baby Blue still didn't look any happier the next day.

"I know what she needs," declared Tigger when he came to visit. "Babies love to be bounced!" Tigger scooped up Baby Blue and took off for a bounce through the Hundred-Acre Wood.

"Oh, do be careful, Tigger," Pooh called after him.

But even after her bounce with Tigger, Baby Blue seemed sad.
So Pooh took her to visit Roo.

"Don't worry. I'll cheer her up," Roo assured Pooh.

Roo took the little blue bird for a ride in his shiny red wagon.

"*Wooo-woooo-woooo!* I'm a fire engine!" yelled Roo.

But Baby Blue still looked sad.

Days passed and Baby Blue didn't get any happier. One afternoon Owl came by for a visit. As soon as Baby Blue saw Owl winging his way toward Pooh's house, the little bird hopped up and down and flapped her wings.

"Look at that!" exclaimed Owl. Then he asked Baby Blue, "Do you want to go flying with Uncle Owl?"

Baby Blue flapped even harder. So Owl took Baby Blue on a swooping and soaring flight above the Hundred-Acre Wood.

After they landed, Owl gently placed Baby Blue on the tip of his wing. "Watch this," Owl told Pooh.

The tiny bird flapped her wings and she began to fly—all by herself!

"Don't go too far, Baby Blue," called Pooh.

Baby Blue looked down and saw that Pooh was worried, so she flew back to join him.

"Now that Baby Blue can fly, maybe she will be happy," said Pooh with a smile.

But that night Baby Blue seemed even sadder than before.
"Think, think, think," said Pooh. "What can I do?"
Early the next morning Pooh took Baby Blue to Owl's house.
Piglet and Tigger came with him.
"You keep her, Owl," Pooh said sadly. "She likes you better."
"Baby Blue likes you very much, Pooh," said Owl. "But she's
a wild bird. She's not meant to live in a house—she's meant to fly.

"Think about it, Pooh," continued Owl. "Could you live on a lily pad like a frog?"

Pooh thought about it. "No, I couldn't," he said.

"And, Piglet, could you live high in a tree like a squirrel?" Owl asked.

Piglet thought about it. "No, I couldn't," he said. "I don't like heights too much."

"And, Tigger, could you sleep upside down in a cave like a bat?" Owl asked.

"No way," said Tigger. "Tiggers hate caves!"

"Well, Baby Blue can't live in Pooh's house, especially now that she's almost grown-up," said Owl. "But you're her friends, and she hates to leave you."

"Oh, but we want Baby Blue to be happy," said Pooh.

So Pooh took Baby Blue to the edge of Owl's porch.

"Go on, Blue. You're not a baby anymore," said Pooh. "I hope you'll be very happy."

"*Cheep,*" Blue said. Then, with a wave of her wing, she flew away, high above the tall treetops of the Hundred-Acre Wood.

"She's happy now," said Pooh with a sigh. "But *I'm* feeling a little blue."

Things were lonely around Pooh's house for several days.
But one morning Pooh was awakened by a beautiful song.

He rushed outside. There was Blue, chirping happily.

She landed on Pooh's shoulder, then flew to a nest above
his head.

"Oh, you've built a nest in my tree!" shouted Pooh.

Blue waved at Pooh. *"Cheep! Cheep! Cheep!"*

Pooh waved back. "Hi, neighbor!"

And both Pooh and Blue felt very happy at last.